Dragonfly KITES
Pimithaagansa

By Tomson Highway
Illustrations by Julie Flett

Tomson Highway oochi
Oos'soopeega-igana Julie Flett oochi

FIFTH
HOUSE

This edition published in Canada by Fifth House Publishers, 2016
Text copyright © 2002 by Tomson Highway
Illustrations copyright © 2016 by Julie Flett

HarperCollins edition published in 2002

Published in Canada by Fifth House Publishers,
195 Allstate Parkway, Markham, Ontario L3R 4T8

Published in the United States by Fifth House Publishers,
311 Washington Street, Brighton, Massachusetts 02135

Fifth House Publishers acknowledges with thanks the Ontario Arts Council for their support
of our publishing program. We acknowledge the financial support of the Government of Canada
through the Canada Book Fund (CBF) for our publishing activities.

Library and Archives Canada Cataloguing in Publication
Highway, Tomson, 1951-, author
Dragonfly kites / by Tomson Highway ; illustrations by Julie Flett = Pimithaagansa /
Tomson Highway oohci ; oos'soopeega-igana Julie Flett oochi.
Previously published: Toronto: HarperCollins, 2002.
Text in English and Cree.
ISBN 978-1-897252-63-5 (bound)
1. Dragonflies--Juvenile fiction. I. Flett, Julie, illustrator II. Title.
III. Title: Pimithaagansa.
PS8565.I433D682 2015   jC813'.54   C2015-905631-4

Publisher Cataloging-in-Publication Data (U.S)
Highway, Tomson, 1951—
Dragonfly kites = Pimithaagansa / by Tomson Highway ;
illustrations by Julie Flett = Tomson Highway oochi ; Oos'soopeega-Igana Julie Flett oochi.
[ ] pages : color illustrations ; cm.
Summary: Dragonfly Kites refers to "kites" made by tying a string around the middles of dragonflies.
Two Cree brothers in northern Manitoba fly these kites during the day, but at night fly themselves in their dreams.
The book is bilingual, written in English and Cree. This is the second book in the Magical Songs of the North Wind trilogy.
ISBN: 978-1-89725-263-5 (pbk.)
1. Kites – Juvenile fiction. 2. Cree children – Canada -- Juvenile fiction.
3. Bilingual books – Juvenile fiction. 4. Dreams – Juvenile fiction. I. Flett, Julie. II. Title.
[E] dc23   PZ7.H544Dr 2015

Cover and text design by Tanya Montini

For the children of Brochet, Manitoba, my hometown.
Awaas'suk Brochet oochi kichi, ita neesta kaa-ootaskiyaan.
– T.H.

For my dad and my uncles, Raymond, Joe and Bruce.
Nipaapaa kichi ooma, meena noogoomisuk Raymond, Joe, igwa Bruce.
– J.F.

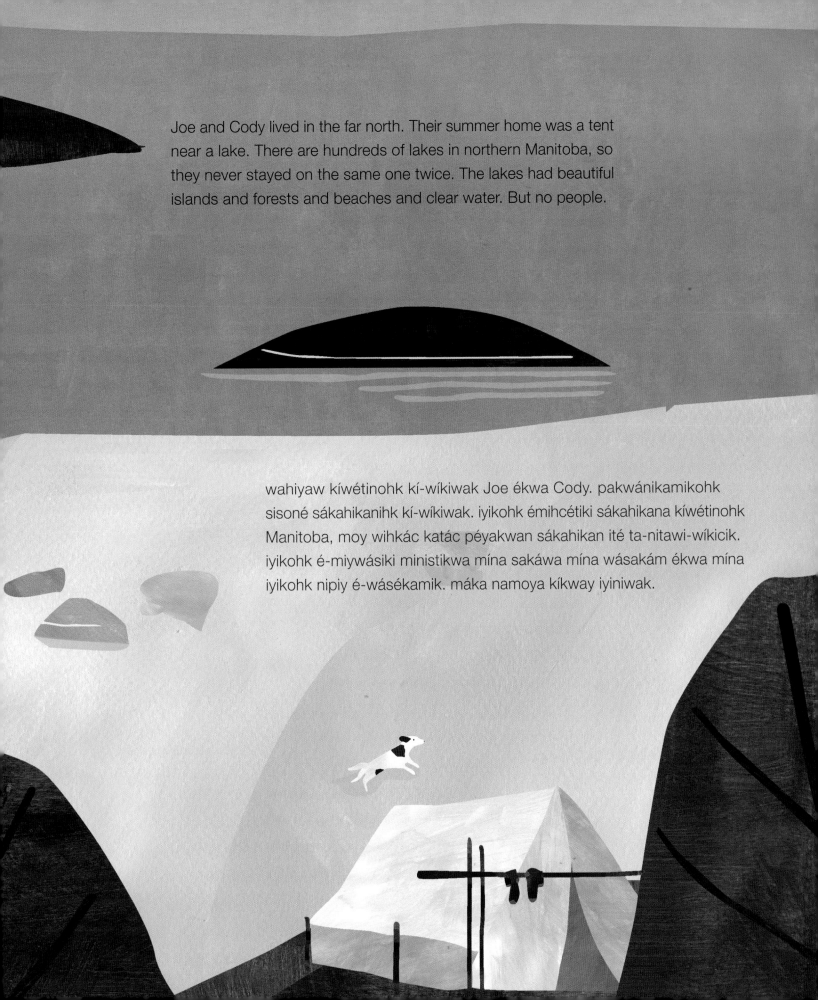

Joe and Cody lived in the far north. Their summer home was a tent near a lake. There are hundreds of lakes in northern Manitoba, so they never stayed on the same one twice. The lakes had beautiful islands and forests and beaches and clear water. But no people.

wahiyaw kíwétinohk kí-wíkiwak Joe ékwa Cody. pakwánikamikohk sisoné sákahikanihk kí-wíkiwak. iyikohk émihcétiki sákahikana kíwétinohk Manitoba, moy wihkác katác péyakwan sákahikan ité ta-nitawi-wíkicik. iyikohk é-miywásiki ministikwa mína sakáwa mína wásakám ékwa mína iyikohk nipiy é-wásékamik. máka namoya kíkway iyiniwak.

There were just Joe and Cody, their papa and their mama—and Cody's little dog, Ootsie, who was almost a person.

Cody ékwa Joe piko ékota kí-wíkiwak asici opápáwáwa ékwa omámáwáwa ékwa Otisiy, Cody océmisisa, mitoni mána iyiniwa é-k-ítéyimácik.

While their parents caught fish, the boys would think up games with made-up toys. They would take a long, thin stick and name it John. They would name another stick Mary. They would name a stone Bobby. Another stone would be called Nancy.

mékwác mána opápáwáwa ékwa omámáwáwa é-pakitahwéyit, aniki níso nápésisak kí-métawéwak mána métawákana wiyawáw tipiyaw é-kí-osihtácik. é-kinwáyik mistik ta-otinamwak ékwa John kí-isiyihkátamwak. kotak mistik Mary kí-isiyihkátamwak. péyak asinísis Bobby é-kí-isiyihkátácik. kotak asinísis Nancy kí-isiyihkátéwak.

They would put John and Bobby and Mary and Nancy in a circle with all
the other sticks and stones they named. They would talk with their
new friends. They would sing and dance. They would even sleep
with the sticks and stones and make them breakfast.

John ékwa Bobby ékwa Mary ékwa Nancy kahkiyaw mámawi
kí-wásakápíhéwak mána asici aniki kotaka mistikwa mína asinísisa
ká-kí-wíhácik. t-ácimostawéwak mána aniki kahkiyaw owícéwákaniwáwa.
kí-nikamowak ékwa kí-nímihitowak mána. ahpo kí-wípéméwak ékwa
kíkisépáyáyiki kí-asaméwak.

One summer, Joe and Cody made a pet of a baby Arctic tern. They called him Freddy. Another summer, their pet was a baby loon named Sally. Sally wasn't very good at walking, but she swam well.

péyakwáw é-nípihk, Joe ékwa Cody ká-kí-ohpikihácik péyak kiyáskosisa. Freddy kí-isiyihkátéwak. kotak mína é-nípiniyik, é-kí-ohpikihácik mákosisa é-apisísisiyit Sally é-kí-isiyihkátácik. namoy kwayask kí-kaskihtáw ta-pimohtét Sally máka kwayask kí-nihtá-pakásimow.

The boys named the squirrels and the rabbits and the chipmunks that
ate from their hands. They even had names for the ants.

nápésisak kí-wíhéwak óki anikwacása, wáposwa ékwa sásákawápiskosa
ocihcíwahk ká-kí-ohci-mícisoyit. ahpo piko éyikosisak kí-wíhéwak.

They once had two baby eagle friends. They named one Migisoo,
which means "eagle" in Cree. The other they named Wagisoo,
which doesn't mean anything but rhymes with Migisoo.

péyak nípin, níso mikisiwak é-apisísisiyit kí-kanawéyiméwak. awa
mikisiw péyak, Mikisiw é-kí-isiyihkátácik ayis ékosi isi itwániwan
ká-néhiyawék. ékwa ana kotak mikisiwa Wákisiw kí-isiyihkátéwak
ayis Mikisiw é-itihtákwák anima wíhowin Mikisiw.

But the dragonflies were their favourite pets.

pimihákanisak máka mána é-kí-máwaci-miyiwéyimácik.

They caught them in a net as the dragonflies flew by the tent. They took pieces of thread from their mother's sewing kit and tied one end gently around the middle of each dragonfly. Joe and Cody held on to the other end of the thread and let the dragonflies go.

ayapiya é-ohci-tápakwátácik pakwánikamikohk ká-kí-pim-pimihácik. asapáp omámáwáwa okaskikwásowatiyiw ohci kí-otinamwak ékwa nisihkác kí-tákopitéwak watáyihk. Joe ékwa Cody kí-miciminamwak mána asapáp ékosi kí-pakitinéwak aniki pimihákanisa.

Off they flew. The brothers ran along behind them. Ootsie ran, too,
jumping and barking.

hé, aspin ká-sipwé-pihácik. ékosi nápésisak kí-pimitisahwéwak mána.
Otisiy wísta kí-pimitisahikéw é-ká-kwáskohtit mína é-mikisimot.

The brothers followed their magic kites through the meadows, past the trees, down to the water, and all along the beach. They ran and ran, until the sun began to set. Then they let go of the strings and waved goodbye to the dragonflies.

aniki napésisak kí-pimitisahwéwak pimihákanisa ita kápaskwáhk, nócimihk, násipétimihk ékwa mína wásakám. ékosi kí-pimpahtáwak iyikohk é-máci-pakisimok. kétahtawé kí-pakitinamwak píminahkwánisa ékosi kí-sipwé-piháwak pimihákanisa.

It was time to go to bed.

piko ékwa ta-kawisimocik.

In their dreams, the boys still ran behind their kites. They ran down the beach and into the water. They hopped from wave to wave. They bounced over islands and leaped over forests. The dragonflies soared high above at the end of long, long strings.

ahpo mékwác é-pawátákik óki nápésisak kéyápic pimitisahikéwak. kí-násipépahtáwak ékwa é-pakastawé-pahtácik. tahkoc é-papamikwáskohticik ká-mámákáskáyik. piko ité é-pásci-ohpíhcik ministikwa ékwa mína sakáwa. ispimihk pimihákanisak pimiháwak píminahkwánisihk kéyápic é-tákopisocik.

Joe and Cody dreamed they jumped so high that they didn't come down.
Off they flew with their dragonfly kites into the gold and pink of the northern
sunset, laughing and laughing. Until it was time to wake up.

Joe ékwa Cody ká-pawátákik iyikohk ispimihk é-is-ohpicik namoy wihkác
káwi-pé-twéhowak. aspin ká-sipwé-pihácik ité ka-máci-pákisimok konita
iyikohk é-pá-pahpicik. isko é-ispayik ta-waniskácik.